To Adèle

J.M.

To Amelia

N.B.

With thanks to
Daphne Elverson
for the use of her
collection of doll's
houses

First published 1993 by Walker Books Ltd
87 Vauxhall Walk, London SE11 5HJ

Text © 1993 Jan Mark
Illustrations © 1993 Nicola Bayley

The right of Jan Mark to be identified as the
author of this work has been asserted by her
in accordance with the Copyright, Designs
and Patents Act 1988.

This book has been set in Berkeley Book.

Printed and bound in Hong Kong by
Dai Nippon Printing Co. (HK) Ltd

British Library Cataloguing in Publication Data
A catalogue record for this book is available
from the British Library.
ISBN 0-7445-2534-9

Fun With Mrs Thumb

Written by

Jan Mark

Illustrated by

Nicola Bayley

WALKER BOOKS
LONDON

Here is the house

and here am I…

And here is
Mrs Thumb.

Mrs Thumb
sits and sews.
Nobody knows
that I have come
to play with Mrs Thumb.

Mrs Thumb,

Mrs Thumb!

Leave your chair

and cross the room.

Let me into

your house.

I will not eat you

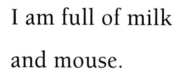

– promise!

I am full of milk

and mouse.

Dear Mrs Thumb,

come out to play.

See what I have

brought today:

my lovely fur,

my lovely purr,

my lovely paws,

full of claws.

Here I come.

Oh, lovely me,

oh, *lucky* Mrs Thumb.

Do you like

hide and seek?

Let's play you're

a mouse –

I'll bite, you squeak.

Off you go!

Bumpety-

bumpety-bump.

I love this game,

aren't you glad I came?

Real mice

squeak and skip

when I nip,

so…

when I pounce,

you bounce.

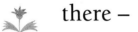
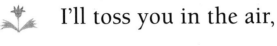

I'll toss you in the air,

there –

why don't you try

to be a bird, and fly?

Now someone's come
to rescue you.
Unfair! Unfair!
They keep doing that
with my mice, too.

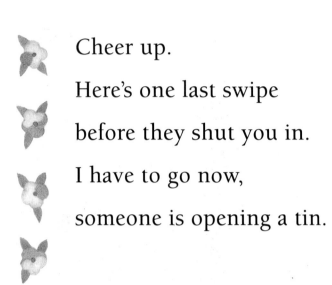

Cheer up.

Here's one last swipe

before they shut you in.

I have to go now,

someone is opening a tin.

Ah, meat is good,
and milk is nice.
That Mrs Thumb is
only made of wood;
unlike mice.

But in a while
I'll go and say
good night to
Mrs Thumb.
I'll look through
the window
of her room
with my smile

and all my lovely teeth.

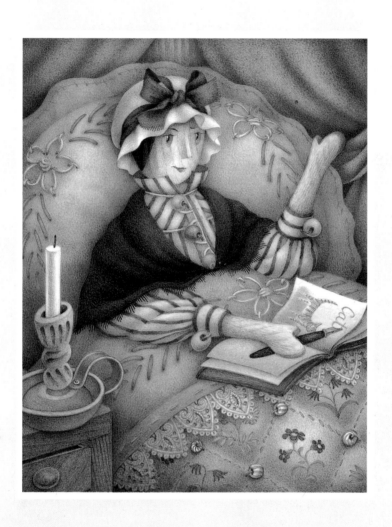